# THE POETRY BUS

## Little Rhymers

Edited By Byron Tobolik

First published in Great Britain in 2022 by:

Young Writers
Remus House
Coltsfoot Drive
Peterborough
PE2 9BF
Telephone: 01733 890066
Website: www.youngwriters.co.uk

All Rights Reserved
Book Design by Ashley Janson
© Copyright Contributors 2021
Softback ISBN 978-1-80015-743-9

Printed and bound in the UK by BookPrintingUK
Website: www.bookprintinguk.com
YB0492B

# Foreword

Welcome to a fun-filled book of poems!

Here at Young Writers, we are delighted to introduce our new poetry competition for KS1 pupils, The Poetry Bus. Pupils could choose to write an acrostic, sense poem or riddle to introduce them to the world of poetry. Giving them this framework allowed the young writers to open their imaginations to a range of topics of their choice, and encouraged them to include other literary techniques such as similes and description.

From family and friends, to animals and places, these pupils have shaped and crafted their ideas brilliantly, showcasing their budding creativity in verse.

We live and breathe creativity here at Young Writers – it gives us life! We want to pass our love of the written word onto the next generation and what better way to do that than to celebrate their writing by publishing it in a book!

Each awesome little poet in this book should be super proud of themselves, and now they've got proof of their imagination and their ideas when they first started creative writing to look back on in years to come! We hope you will delight in these poems as much as we have.

# Contents

**Corpus Christi Catholic Primary School, Boscombe**

| | |
|---|---|
| Roma Ziolko Laszko (5) | 1 |
| Karol Marszalek (5) | 2 |
| Jessica Haddon-Cave (5) | 3 |
| Harvey Webster (5) | 4 |
| Freya Searle (5) | 5 |
| Chizaram Chukuma (6) | 6 |
| Joshua Greir (5) | 7 |
| Maya Smith (6) | 8 |
| Max Korcagins (6) | 9 |
| Florence Garegnani (5) | 10 |
| Miruna Curca (5) | 11 |
| Hannah Mendak (5) | 12 |
| Hanna Halik (5) | 13 |
| Dominik Skierkowski (6) | 14 |
| Leon Wrzesniewski (6) | 15 |
| Cassi Schneider (5) | 16 |
| Lucia Laserna Garcia (5) | 17 |
| Nima Oshima (5) | 18 |
| Aron Piwko (5) | 19 |
| Enoch Ban (5) | 20 |
| Alessandra Dobrescu (5) | 21 |
| Gabriel Vargas (5) | 22 |
| Evie Barr (5) | 23 |
| Razvan Boboc (5) | 24 |
| Zoe Kapitan (6) | 25 |
| Matilda Hickson (5) | 26 |
| Theo Clancy (5) | 27 |
| Sabine Rebollido (6) | 28 |
| Luena Gouveia (5) | 29 |
| Misha Mullally (6) | 30 |
| Matilda Romero (5) | 31 |
| Rafael Trancoso (5) | 32 |
| Elliot Ingleton (5) | 33 |
| Leni-Rae McCormack (6) | 34 |
| Henrique Botelho (5) | 35 |
| Mason Sousa (5) | 36 |

**English Martyrs Primary School, Tilehurst**

| | |
|---|---|
| Macy Onime (6) | 37 |
| Viktor Z (7) | 38 |
| Milena Kitka (6) | 39 |
| Daniel Emami (6) | 40 |
| Milo ML (7) | 41 |
| Lucas K (6) | 42 |
| Michael Opoku (6) | 43 |
| Arya S (6) | 44 |
| Alex K (6) | 45 |
| Lavin Sharma (6) | 46 |
| Christabel F (6) | 47 |
| Emily Stannard (6) | 48 |
| Nikolai P (6) | 49 |
| Maja (6) | 50 |
| Sienna Owusu (6) | 51 |
| Iris B (6) | 52 |
| Emil Pachny (6) | 53 |
| Freya M (7) | 54 |
| Iphigenia Konstantina Iakovidou (6) | 55 |
| Jasper J (6) | 56 |
| Cherilyn Charles Binny (6) | 57 |
| Wylan Amos Ramirez (7) | 58 |
| Judah Bradley (6) | 59 |
| Dominic W (6) | 60 |
| Ronnie-James S (6) | 61 |
| Karol B (6) | 62 |
| Julian W (6) | 63 |
| Jacob A (6) | 64 |

| | |
|---|---|
| Thenul K (7) | 65 |
| Ava Jane Thomas-Nelson (6) | 66 |
| Alexis Cashman (7) | 67 |
| Evan Abieza (6) | 68 |
| Shiena H (7) | 69 |
| Archie Flower (6) | 70 |
| Marcel Callender-Laffin (6) | 71 |
| Finnley S (6) | 72 |
| Daniel Neczaj (6) | 73 |

## North Mymms St Marys CE Primary School, North Mymms

| | |
|---|---|
| Tallulah Harrison (6) | 74 |
| Cristianna Stanley (6) | 75 |
| Olivia-May Roskilly (6) | 76 |
| Izzy Urwin-Scott | 77 |
| James Lown | 78 |
| Nancy (5) | 79 |
| Dennis-Junior Scully (6) | 80 |
| Matthew Langley | 81 |
| Sofia Secara (7) | 82 |
| Daisy Barnes-Welling (5) | 83 |
| Diana Niemyjska (5) | 84 |
| Chanko Chernev (5) | 85 |
| Bella Lown | 86 |
| Freddie Hutchison (5) | 87 |

## Northview Primary School, Neasden

| | |
|---|---|
| Liri Kuka (6) | 88 |
| Firoze Ahmed (6) | 89 |
| Bazail Khan (6) | 90 |
| Taylor Dimitrov (6) | 91 |
| Mariyah Lateef (6) | 92 |
| Renee Amiae Allen (7) | 93 |
| Ahmad Salahi (7) | 94 |
| Mia Vaneva (6) | 95 |
| Isaiah Allen (7) | 96 |
| Simar Mandair (6) | 97 |
| Thierry Safi (6) | 98 |
| Mukti Gami (5) | 99 |
| Almaas Ali (6) | 100 |

| | |
|---|---|
| Adana Samie-Barrett-Williams (6) | 101 |
| Reem Daabaj (6) | 102 |
| Ibrahim Mahamud (6) | 103 |

## Oakdale Primary School, Stanground

| | |
|---|---|
| Teddy Scott (5) | 104 |
| Olivia Firth (5) | 105 |
| Ilaria Nigro (5) | 106 |
| Nate Holmes (6) | 107 |
| Abigail Wisniewski (5) | 108 |
| Jasmine Bentley (5) | 109 |
| Annalise King (5) | 110 |
| Scarlett Briston (5) | 111 |
| Dheeptha Manoj (5) | 112 |
| Mia Garwell (5) | 113 |
| Amelie Monteforte (5) | 114 |
| Erin Skipp (5) | 115 |
| Molly Patten (5) | 116 |

## Penruddock Primary School, Penruddock

| | |
|---|---|
| Jake Nicholson (7) | 117 |
| Ella Platt (7) | 118 |
| Matilda (5) | 119 |
| Eddie Seel (7) | 120 |
| Ted Ware (6) | 121 |
| Dylan Offin (5) | 122 |
| Lily-Ella Biggs (6) | 123 |
| Ed O'Neil (7) | 124 |
| Lewis Nicholson (5) | 125 |
| Jordan Edmondson (6) | 126 |
| Faith Fry (5) | 127 |
| Jos Platt (6) | 128 |
| Joseph Parker (6) | 129 |
| Isaac (6) | 130 |

**St Anthony's Catholic Primary School, Anerley**

Shiloh Marshall (8) 131
Irentoluwa Murphy (7) 132
Lola Harding (7) 134

# Autumn

I can see squirrels charging around,
I can hear cars driving around the city,
I can feel leaves,
I can smell the bonfire,
I can taste hot chocolate with marshmallows.

**Roma Ziolko Laszko (5)**
Corpus Christi Catholic Primary School, Boscombe

# Autumn

I can see the leaves falling,
I can hear crunchy leaves,
I can feel a squirrel's fur,
I can smell toffee apples,
I can see steamy hot chocolate.

### Karol Marszalek (5)
Corpus Christi Catholic Primary School, Boscombe

# Autumn

I can see red leaves,
I can hear crunchy leaves,
I can hear swishy leaves,
I can see soft leaves,
I can see bonfires,
I can see blackberries.

**Jessica Haddon-Cave (5)**
Corpus Christi Catholic Primary School, Boscombe

# Autumn

I can see colourful leaves,
I can hear squirrels in the bushes,
I can feel spiky conkers,
I can smell a warm campfire,
I can taste hot chocolate.

**Harvey Webster (5)**
Corpus Christi Catholic Primary School, Boscombe

# Autumn

I can see falling leaves,
I can hear bonfires and it is hot,
I can feel the rain on my head,
I can smell cute apples,
I can taste my food.

**Freya Searle (5)**
Corpus Christi Catholic Primary School, Boscombe

# Autumn

I can see apples and leaves,
I can hear crunchy leaves,
I can feel mittens,
I can smell the rain and the wind,
I can taste hot coffee.

## Chizaram Chukuma (6)
Corpus Christi Catholic Primary School, Boscombe

# Autumn

I can see leaves sinking,
I can hear the birds singing,
I can see conkers,
I can smell the leaves,
I can taste blackberries.

## Joshua Greir (5)
Corpus Christi Catholic Primary School, Boscombe

# Autumn

I can see colourful leaves,
I can hear birds singing,
I can feel spiky conkers,
I can smell blackberries,
I can taste smoke.

## Maya Smith (6)
Corpus Christi Catholic Primary School, Boscombe

# Autumn

I can see a pumpkin,
I can hear the rain,
I can feel soft leaves,
I can smell hot chocolate,
I can taste sweet blackberries.

**Max Korcagins (6)**
Corpus Christi Catholic Primary School, Boscombe

# Autumn

I can see birds flapping,
I can hear the rain,
I can feel bugs crawling,
I can smell blackberries,
I can taste strawberries.

## Florence Garegnani (5)
Corpus Christi Catholic Primary School, Boscombe

# Autumn Conkers

I can see lots of trees,
I can hear crunchy leaves,
I can feel conkers,
I can smell hot chocolate,
I can taste warm food.

**Miruna Curca (5)**
Corpus Christi Catholic Primary School, Boscombe

# Autumn Conkers

I can see a brown squirrel,
I can hear raindrops,
I can smell toffee apples,
I can feel conkers,
I can taste bonfires.

## Hannah Mendak (5)
Corpus Christi Catholic Primary School, Boscombe

# Autumn

I can see noisy birds,
I can hear cheeky kids,
I can feel fluffy feathers,
I can smell hot cocoa,
I can taste soup.

## Hanna Halik (5)
Corpus Christi Catholic Primary School, Boscombe

# Autumn

I can see red leaves,
I can hear the rain,
I can feel the leaves,
I can smell the flowers,
I can taste the coffee.

**Dominik Skierkowski (6)**
Corpus Christi Catholic Primary School, Boscombe

# Autumn

I can see a squirrel,
I can hear leaves,
I can feel bonfires,
I can smell toffee apples,
I can taste blackberries.

## Leon Wrzesniewski (6)
Corpus Christi Catholic Primary School, Boscombe

# Autumn

I can see brown leaves,
I can hear squirrels squeaking,
I can taste yummy, hot chicken soup,
I can smell hot chocolate.

**Cassi Schneider (5)**
Corpus Christi Catholic Primary School, Boscombe

# Autumn

I can see noisy squirrels,
I can feel warm jumpers,
I can smell soup,
I can taste blackberries,
I can hear cars.

**Lucia Laserna Garcia (5)**
Corpus Christi Catholic Primary School, Boscombe

# Autumn

I can see crunchy leaves,
I can hear leaves,
I can feel conkers,
I can smell yummy food,
I can taste warm food.

## Nima Oshima (5)
Corpus Christi Catholic Primary School, Boscombe

# Autumn

I can see colourful leaves,
I can hear the birds,
I can see conkers,
I can smell the rain,
I can taste coffee.

**Aron Piwko (5)**
Corpus Christi Catholic Primary School, Boscombe

# Autumn

I can see conkers,
I can hear the birds,
I can smell good food,
I can feel the trees,
I can taste red berries.

**Enoch Ban (5)**
Corpus Christi Catholic Primary School, Boscombe

# Autumn

I can see red leaves,
I can hear leaves falling down,
I can feel leaves,
I can smell coffee,
I can taste food.

**Alessandra Dobrescu (5)**
Corpus Christi Catholic Primary School, Boscombe

# Autumn

I can see flowers,
I can hear squirrels,
I can feel toffee apples,
I can smell the rain,
I can taste pumpkins.

**Gabriel Vargas (5)**
Corpus Christi Catholic Primary School, Boscombe

# Autumn

I can see leaves,
I can see squirrels,
I can hear crunchy leaves,
I can see trees,
I can smell hot chocolate.

## Evie Barr (5)
Corpus Christi Catholic Primary School, Boscombe

# Autumn

I can see leaves,
I can hear squirrels,
I can feel crunchy leaves,
I can smell the rain,
I can taste fruit.

## Razvan Boboc (5)
Corpus Christi Catholic Primary School, Boscombe

# Autumn

I can see toffee apples,
I can hear squirrels,
I can feel conkers,
I can smell leaves,
I can taste coffee.

**Zoe Kapitan (6)**
Corpus Christi Catholic Primary School, Boscombe

# Autumn

I can see conkers,
I can hear the birds,
I can feel leaves,
I can smell cats,
I can taste the sky.

**Matilda Hickson (5)**
Corpus Christi Catholic Primary School, Boscombe

# Autumn

I can see leaves,
I can hear squirrels screaming,
I can feel soft mittens,
I can smell hot chocolate.

**Theo Clancy (5)**
Corpus Christi Catholic Primary School, Boscombe

# Things You Can See In Autumn

I can see smoke,
I can feel bumpy tree logs,
I can smell autumn leaves,
I can taste marshmallows.

### Sabine Rebollido (6)
Corpus Christi Catholic Primary School, Boscombe

# Autumn

I can see conkers,
I can hear cars,
I can feel conkers,
I can smell soup
I can taste soup.

## Luena Gouveia (5)
Corpus Christi Catholic Primary School, Boscombe

# Autumn

I can see cars,
I can hear a cat,
I can feel a cat,
I can smell flowers,
I can taste soup.

## Misha Mullally (6)
Corpus Christi Catholic Primary School, Boscombe

# Autumn

I can see falling leaves,
I can hear the loud rain,
I can feel soft leaves,
I can smell soup.

## Matilda Romero (5)
Corpus Christi Catholic Primary School, Boscombe

# Autumn

I can see mittens,
I can hear bonfires,
I can feel bonfires,
I can smell leaves and rain.

**Rafael Trancoso (5)**
Corpus Christi Catholic Primary School, Boscombe

# Autumn

I can see a squirrel's soft fur,
I can feel crunchy leaves,
I can see spiky conkers.

**Elliot Ingleton (5)**
Corpus Christi Catholic Primary School, Boscombe

# Autumn

I can see leaves,
I can hear birds,
I can feel spikes,
I can smell pumpkins.

## Leni-Rae McCormack (6)
Corpus Christi Catholic Primary School, Boscombe

# Autumn

I can see...
Squirrels,
Falling leaves,
The rain,
Marshmallows.

### Henrique Botelho (5)
Corpus Christi Catholic Primary School, Boscombe

# Autumn

I can see pumpkins,
I can hear a noisy squirrel,
I can feel soft mittens.

**Mason Sousa (5)**
Corpus Christi Catholic Primary School, Boscombe

# Cinderella

**C** inderella is a sweet girl
**I** t is a sunny beautiful day
**N** ext day, Cinderella made breakfast
**D** ay three, Cinderella saw a poster to go to a ball
**E** nd of the night, her slipper fell off
**R** an home - the spell wore off
**E** very night, Cinderella cried
**L** ast day, Cinderella saw the prince. She was locked up in her room
**L** ittle mice unlocked her door
**A** prince tried the last princess and the prince kissed Cinderella.

## Macy Onime (6)
English Martyrs Primary School, Tilehurst

# Football

**F** ootball is my favourite thing to do. When I play, I do amazingly
**O** nly my team win games
**O** nly a best friend will know that I like football
**T** he team that I love is Arsenal because I love the red and white kits
**B** eckham is my favourite player
**A** very good player, his kits are smooth
**L** uck to my team
**L** uck to the other teams.

**Viktor Z (7)**
English Martyrs Primary School, Tilehurst

# Happiness

Happiness is seeing my mum,
Happiness is feeling my little cat because it is furry, soft and lovely,
Happiness is hearing my favourite song - any song that I can,
Happiness is smelling the nice, humongous cake,
Happiness is tasting my favourite fruit and food,
Happiness is the colour blue because it is my favourite.

**Milena Kitka (6)**
English Martyrs Primary School, Tilehurst

# Football

**F** ootballers have got bumpy shoes
**O** range ball goes in the goal
**O** r the football misses
**T** ackling players try to get the ball
**B** lack kit on the striker
**A** lways try to win
**L** ike to get a goal
**L** ightning-speed runners.

**Daniel Emami (6)**
English Martyrs Primary School, Tilehurst

# Movies

M agic movies in the dark!
O ther people are scared but some are not
V isitors can sometimes be villains but some are good
I like movies, they are fun
"E nd of the movie!" I sometimes say
S ad when it ends, it was fun watching.

## Milo ML (7)
English Martyrs Primary School, Tilehurst

# Happiness

Happiness is seeing a sparkly picture,
Happiness is feeling my baby sister,
Happiness is hearing my mummy's laughter,
Happiness is smelling a big sprinkle-covered cake,
Happiness is tasting fish and a big bag of chips,
Happiness is the colour red because it is for love.

**Lucas K (6)**
English Martyrs Primary School, Tilehurst

# Fear

Fear is seeing red fire,
Fear is feeling a big spider run up your arm,
Fear is hearing a scary noise,
Fear is tasting blue cheese for the first time,
Fear is seeing a monster,
Fear is what you feel when you are in trouble,
Have you ever felt fear before?

**Michael Opoku (6)**
English Martyrs Primary School, Tilehurst

# What Am I?

Inside me, you can find jellyfish and sharks,
Sometimes I find pirates above me,
I am blue and sapphire,
I like to crash,
People like me,
Sometimes I am dirty because people throw rubbish in me,
What am I?

Answer: I am the ocean.

## Arya S (6)
English Martyrs Primary School, Tilehurst

# Minecraft

**M** inecraft is my favourite game
**I** love the Minecraft dogs
**N** ight-time, darkness comes...
**E** nder dragon
**C** reeper
**R** ailway tracks
**A** ll the pigs
**F** all into the sea
**T** o find a squid.

## Alex K (6)
English Martyrs Primary School, Tilehurst

# Who Am I?

My favourite food is cheese sandwiches,
I have black and brown eyes,
I am always grumpy,
I would love to drive a Lamborghini car,
One of my teeth has gone,
My favourite animal is a cheetah.
Who am I?

Answer: I am Lavin.

## Lavin Sharma (6)
English Martyrs Primary School, Tilehurst

# Happiness

Happiness is seeing a fluffy dog,
Happiness is feeling furry cats,
Happiness is hearing my mother's voice,
Happiness is smelling humongous flowers,
Happiness is tasting salty food,
Happiness is the colour pink because it's my favourite.

## Christabel F (6)
English Martyrs Primary School, Tilehurst

# Who Am I?

I have two sparkly blue eyes,
My favourite food is macaroni cheese,
My hair is blonde,
I like to play with dogs,
I am kind and helpful to others,
My favourite headband is my rabbit one.
Who am I?

*Answer: I am Emily.*

## Emily Stannard (6)
English Martyrs Primary School, Tilehurst

# Minecraft

**M** inecraft
**I** s the best
**N** ow I play on the PS5
**E** asy to play
**C** rafting a diamond pickaxe
**R** unning to a house to hide from zombies
**A** car to drive
**F** ar away
**T** o the beach.

**Nikolai P (6)**
English Martyrs Primary School, Tilehurst

# Sadness

Sadness is a dog that is wet,
Sadness is feeling upset when you have no friends,
Sadness is hearing a baby crying,
Sadness is smelling the rain,
Sadness is tasting tears from your eyes,
Sadness is the colour black because it is dark.

## Maja (6)
English Martyrs Primary School, Tilehurst

# Parrot

**P** arts of me can fly
**A** nd I live in the forest
**R** eally like to eat seeds
**R** ed is one of the colours on my feathers
**O** live trees are my favourite to make my nest in
**T** rees have twigs for my nest.

## Sienna Owusu (6)
English Martyrs Primary School, Tilehurst

# Happiness

Happiness is seeing the sun,
Happiness is feeling my soft cat,
Happiness is hearing the cold wind,
Happiness is smelling wrapping paper,
Happiness is tasting food from Mr Cod,
Happiness is the colour pink because I love pigs.

**Iris B (6)**
English Martyrs Primary School, Tilehurst

# Happiness

Happiness is seeing my friends listening to me,
Happiness is feeling a flower,
Happiness is hearing a beautiful sound,
Happiness is smelling my pet cat,
Happiness is tasting fish and chips,
Happiness is the colour pink.

**Emil Pachny (6)**
English Martyrs Primary School, Tilehurst

# Happiness

Happiness is seeing stars in the sky,
Happiness is feeling my toys,
Happiness is hearing Mummy sing,
Happiness is smelling fresh hot dogs,
Happiness is tasting cheese pizza,
Happiness is the colour red for a heart.

**Freya M (7)**
English Martyrs Primary School, Tilehurst

# Who Am I?

I have a cat headband,
My favourite food is soup,
My cat makes me happy,
I have one braid,
My favourite thing to do is colouring,
My cat likes to play games.
Who am I?

Answer: I am Iphi.

## Iphigenia Konstantina Iakovidou (6)
English Martyrs Primary School, Tilehurst

# Happiness

Happiness is seeing a warm hug,
Happiness is feeling a marshmallow,
Happiness is hearing a circus,
Happiness is smelling a big cake,
Happiness is tasting a cookie,
Happiness is the colour gold like the sunshine.

**Jasper J (6)**
English Martyrs Primary School, Tilehurst

# Happiness

Happiness is a blue sea,
Happiness is feeling my cosy bed,
Happiness is hearing calm music,
Happiness is smelling my birthday cake,
Happiness is tasting sugar,
Happiness is the colour blue for the sea.

## Cherilyn Charles Binny (6)
English Martyrs Primary School, Tilehurst

# What Am I?

My fin is smooth,
I cannot be kept as a pet,
You can find me in the cold blue sea,
My colours are black and blue,
Tasty fish is my favourite food.
What am I?

Answer: I am a whale.

## Wylan Amos Ramirez (7)
English Martyrs Primary School, Tilehurst

# Happiness

Happiness is seeing sweets,
Happiness is feeling my mummy,
Happiness is hearing snoring,
Happiness is smelling green grass,
Happiness is tasting sweets,
Happiness is the colour green for grass.

**Judah Bradley (6)**
English Martyrs Primary School, Tilehurst

# Happiness

Happiness is seeing my pet,
Happiness is feeling a big cake,
Happiness is hearing calm music,
Happiness is smelling flowers,
Happiness is tasting chocolate,
Happiness is the colour of grass.

**Dominic W (6)**
English Martyrs Primary School, Tilehurst

# Fear

Fear is seeing black bats,
Fear is feeling a poisonous spider,
Fear is hearing footsteps,
Fear is smelling rotten pizza,
Fear is tasting rotten sandwiches,
Fear is the colour red for blood.

**Ronnie-James S (6)**
English Martyrs Primary School, Tilehurst

# Fear

Fear is seeing scary faces,
Fear is feeling sharp teeth,
Fear is hearing scary footsteps,
Fear is smelling liquid blood,
Fear is tasting rotten doughnuts,
Fear is the colour red for blood.

**Karol B (6)**
English Martyrs Primary School, Tilehurst

# Who Am I?

Painting is my favourite,
I don't wear big glasses,
Singing is my favourite,
My favourite food is noodles,
I like reading.
Who am I?

Answer: I am Julian.

## Julian W (6)
English Martyrs Primary School, Tilehurst

# Who Am I?

My favourite animal is a sausage dog,
I have bright blonde hair,
My favourite food is pizza,
My favourite thing to do is paint.
Who am I?

*Answer: I am Jacob.*

## Jacob A (6)
English Martyrs Primary School, Tilehurst

# Who Am I?

My eye colour is brown,
My hair colour is black,
My favourite food is a carrot,
I was born in the month of August.
Who am I?

Answer: I am Thenul.

**Thenul K (7)**
English Martyrs Primary School, Tilehurst

# Who Am I?

My eye colour is brown,
My hair colour is brown,
My favourite food is doughnuts,
I was born in the month of May.
Who am I?

Answer: I am Ava Jane.

## Ava Jane Thomas-Nelson (6)
English Martyrs Primary School, Tilehurst

# What Am I?

My colours are black and yellow,
I am very big,
I make you happy,
You can play with me,
I am a game.
What am I?

*Answer: I am Roblox.*

**Alexis Cashman (7)**
English Martyrs Primary School, Tilehurst

# The Ocean

O cean is blue
C oral lives at the bottom of the ocean
E els sting
A ngelfish hide in a cave
N oisy submarines in the ocean.

## Evan Abieza (6)
English Martyrs Primary School, Tilehurst

# Who Am I?

I have two brown eyes,
My favourite food is pizza,
My friend has kind hands,
I wear a hairband.
Who am I?

*Answer: I am Shiena.*

## Shiena H (7)
English Martyrs Primary School, Tilehurst

# Who Am I?

My hair is short and brown,
My eyes are green,
Yummy corn is my favourite,
I love dogs.
Who am I?

Answer: I am Archie.

## Archie Flower (6)
English Martyrs Primary School, Tilehurst

# Jack

**J** ack and the Beanstalk
**A** t the top was a giant
**C** limbing up the beanstalk
**K** nocked down, the giant crashed.

**Marcel Callender-Laffin (6)**
English Martyrs Primary School, Tilehurst

# Who Am I?

My hair is short and blonde,
My eyes are blue,
My favourite animal is a rabbit.
Who am I?

Answer: I am Finnley.

## Finnley S (6)
English Martyrs Primary School, Tilehurst

# Bugs

**B** ees buzzing
**U** p in the sky
**G** oing high
**S** unny day.

## Daniel Neczaj (6)
English Martyrs Primary School, Tilehurst

# Autumn

**A** nimals are trying to find shelter, so they are not cold
**U** nder the trees, the orange, red and gold leaves drop down on the green grass
**T** he conkers start to fall down and may cause a bang on the frosty ground
**U** nder the pouring rain, so your umbrella gets wet
**M** arshmallows are nice when I watch the fireworks
**N** ights are long and dark.

**Tallulah Harrison (6)**
North Mymms St Marys CE Primary School, North Mymms

# Autumn

**A** nimals are getting ready to go and get some food
**U** mbrellas are good for us because we put them up
**T** he bonfires are for us because they are fun and we laugh
**U** nder the trees, me, my dad and my mum laugh together
**M** y dad put the fireworks on. Pop! It went so far!
**N** ext, we got hot chocolate. It was yum!

## Cristianna Stanley (6)
North Mymms St Marys CE Primary School, North Mymms

# Autumn

**A** nimals are getting ready for winter
**U** mbrellas are good for you because they protect you from the pouring rain
**T** he fireworks are beautiful
**U** nder the trees leaves fall and I crunch and walk on them
**M** arshmallows and hot cocoa is yummy
**N** ights are dark, long and cold.

**Olivia-May Roskilly (6)**
North Mymms St Marys CE Primary School, North Mymms

# Autumn

**A** nimals are getting ready to hibernate
**U** nder the trees I watch the fireworks go pop and bang
**T** he hot chocolate is yummy and delicious. We are so cosy and warm
**U** mbrellas keep us dry from the heavy rain
**M** ummy takes me to see the fireworks
**N** ights are long and dark.

## Izzy Urwin-Scott
North Mymms St Marys CE Primary School, North Mymms

# Autumn

I can see red and green apples falling from the trees for me to catch in my hands
I can hear the wind blowing the leaves around
I can feel the slime on the dark brown conkers on the ground
I can taste apples and pears and oranges
I can smell fireworks and sausages.

**James Lown**
North Mymms St Marys CE Primary School, North Mymms

# Autumn

I can see twirly red leaves on the ground
I can hear fireworks going *boom, boom, boom*
I can feel the ice-cold wind blowing my hair into my face
I can taste yummy Halloween treats
I can smell fireworks on fire.

## Nancy (5)
North Mymms St Marys CE Primary School, North Mymms

# Autumn

**A** nimals are getting ready for winter,
**U** mbrellas for when it rains
**T** he bonfires bash and boom
**U** nder the trees, leaves fall
**M** arshmallows are nice
**N** ights are dark.

### Dennis-Junior Scully (6)
North Mymms St Marys CE Primary School, North Mymms

# Autumn

I can see fireworks flashing in the sky
I can hear leaves going *crunch, crunch crunch*
I can feel the wind vortexing
I can taste burgers and milk
I can smell yummy food cooking in the oven.

## Matthew Langley
North Mymms St Marys CE Primary School, North Mymms

# Autumn

**A** nimals go to sleep
**U** mbrella when it is raining
**T** he weather is chilly
**U** nder trees leaves fall
**M** any colours around
**N** ights are dark.

## Sofia Secara (7)
North Mymms St Marys CE Primary School, North Mymms

# Autumn

I can see brown leaves falling from the trees
I can hear fireworks popping in the sky
I can feel leaves falling from the sky
I can taste the pumpkin pie
I can smell pumpkins.

### Daisy Barnes-Welling (5)
North Mymms St Marys CE Primary School, North Mymms

# Autumn

I can see fireworks shooting in the sky
I can hear *crack, bang, pop*
I can feel warm and cosy
I can taste marshmallows
I can smell bonfire.

## Diana Niemyjska (5)
North Mymms St Marys CE Primary School, North Mymms

# Autumn

I can see big fireworks
I can hear the birds in the sky
I can feel the leaves when I pick them up
I can taste pasta
I can smell cake.

## Chanko Chernev (5)
North Mymms St Marys CE Primary School, North Mymms

# Autumn

I can see orange and yellow leaves
I can hear the wind
I can feel the ran
I can taste sausages
I can smell fireworks.

## Bella Lown
North Mymms St Marys CE Primary School, North Mymms

# Autumn

I can see leaves everywhere
I can hear fireworks
I can feel cold wind
I can taste yummy food
I can smell the bonfire.

### Freddie Hutchison (5)
North Mymms St Marys CE Primary School, North Mymms

# At The Beach

I love the beach,
The beach is the best,
I love it, it's the best!
I love the beach,
Because it is hot,
That means we can have ice cream,
And we can eat stretchy ice cream,
And drink Coca-Cola,
And other cold drinks and food.
I can see the sea,
And I can feel the warmth,
I can smell seaweed,
I can taste yummy hot dogs.

## Liri Kuka (6)
Northview Primary School, Neasden

# Going On Planes

When I go on my trip,
I can see the water drip,
I see the clouds that are thick,
But have no fear because it's a trick,
I can hear the bell ring,
As I sit here and sing,
But then I set off,
Without a cough,
With the knowledge that I've put into your brain,
See for yourselves what's in a plane!

**Firoze Ahmed (6)**
Northview Primary School, Neasden

# At The Beach

I can hear the sea,
I can see the water,
I can smell the barbecue,
I can taste the barbecue,
I can feel the sand,
I can see the crabs,
I can feel the water,
I can hear the birds,
I can still hear the sea,
I can taste the ice cream,
I can hear the crabs,
I can taste the chocolate.

## Bazail Khan (6)
Northview Primary School, Neasden

# Summer

I can see food,
I can hear people making friends,
I can see people at the seaside,
I can smell flames,
I can see a lot of stuff,
I can see fruit,
I can feel bananas,
I like the food,
I like to eat my food,
I play a lot,
I can taste hot chocolate,
I like my hot chocolate.

**Taylor Dimitrov (6)**
Northview Primary School, Neasden

# At The Beach

I can see the waves glistening,
I can hear the seagulls squawking,
I can feel the sand getting stuck to my toes,
I can taste cold strawberry ice cream,
I can smell the salty water,
And I can smell food that is hot dogs,
I can see people standing,
Oh, I love the beach!

**Mariyah Lateef (6)**
Northview Primary School, Neasden

# My Trip To America

I can see rainbow butterflies,
I can feel the breeze blowing in the air,
I can hear the bees buzzing,
I can taste the Oreos in my mouth,
I can smell the flowers,
Oh, how I love my grandma so much!

**Renee Amiae Allen (7)**
Northview Primary School, Neasden

# At The Pool

I can see the water,
I can hear the people splashing in the water,
I can feel the warm water,
I can taste the bleachy water,
I can smell the chlorine from the water,
Oh, how I like the pool!

**Ahmad Salahi (7)**
Northview Primary School, Neasden

# I Love School

I can hear people chatting,
I can feel me writing with a pencil,
I can smell flowers outside,
I can taste tasty lunch,
I can see interesting books around me,
I love all of those things.

## Mia Vaneva (6)
Northview Primary School, Neasden

# The Swimming Pool

I can feel the water in my hands,
I can smell the fresh air,
I can taste the water,
I can see the lifeguards helping people,
I can hear the bird tweeting,
I love swimming!

**Isaiah Allen (7)**
Northview Primary School, Neasden

# At The Beach

I can smell the fish,
I can feel the soft sand,
I can see the waves crashing,
I can hear the seagulls,
I can taste the salty water,
Oh, how I love the beach so much!

**Simar Mandair (6)**
Northview Primary School, Neasden

# The Beach

I can see the sea,
I can hear the seagulls,
I can feel the rough sand,
I can taste the chips,
I can smell the fishy smell of the sea,
The beach is the best!

**Thierry Safi (6)**
Northview Primary School, Neasden

# Butterfly

Butterfly fell and bruised her leg,
So she was very sad,
But she didn't care,
So she carried on walking,
Her leg got better,
So she flew away to play.

**Mukti Gami (5)**
Northview Primary School, Neasden

# Eid

I can see the masjid,
I can hear Asha,
I can feel the carpet,
I can smell the tasty food,
I can taste the yummy chocolates,
Eid is the best festival!

## Almaas Ali (6)
Northview Primary School, Neasden

# River

**R**ivers are calm
**I** like rivers
**V** ery smooth
**E** xciting to see
**R** ivers can be called a stream or creek.

**Adana Samie-Barrett-Williams (6)**
Northview Primary School, Neasden

# The Beach

I can see the ice cream van,
Mum likes the beach,
Dad likes the beach,
I like to eat yummy food,
It is so yummy!

## Reem Daabaj (6)
Northview Primary School, Neasden

# In Somalia

I can see Somalia,
And all the beautiful stuff,
And when I am at home,
I pray that I can see it again.

**Ibrahim Mahamud (6)**
Northview Primary School, Neasden

# Planes

**P** lanes can be gold
**L** ike a bird
**A** ll the dust that they kick up
**N** ot on the sea
**E** very day, they rescue people
**S** oar in the dark night-time.

## Teddy Scott (5)
Oakdale Primary School, Stanground

# Planes

**P** lanes can zoom and fly
**L** ike a bird and an eagle
**A** ll over the world
**N** ot on the land and the beach
**E** very day
**S** eeing the bright sun.

## Olivia Firth (5)
Oakdale Primary School, Stanground

# Planes

**P** lanes can whoosh off
**L** ike a bee
**A** ll over the sky
**N** ot on the land
**E** very plane has wheels
**S** oar high in the sky.

## Ilaria Nigro (5)
Oakdale Primary School, Stanground

# Planes

**P** lanes can fly
**L** ike an eagle
**A** ll over the sky
**N** ot on the sea
**E** veryone has to fly
**S** oar in the blue sky.

## Nate Holmes (6)
Oakdale Primary School, Stanground

# Plane

**P** lanes can drive
**L** ike a bus but it flies
**A** ll over the world
**N** ot on the sea
**E** very day, it soars into the sun.

## Abigail Wisniewski (5)
Oakdale Primary School, Stanground

# Plane

**P** lanes fly in the sky
**L** ike a moth
**A** nd like a butterfly
**N** o one is flying
**E** ngine is pink.

**Jasmine Bentley (5)**
Oakdale Primary School, Stanground

# Boats

**B** oats can float
**O** n the water
**A** nd they have sails
**T** o sail to different countries.

**Annalise King (5)**
Oakdale Primary School, Stanground

# Cars

**C** ars have wheels
**A** ll have axles
**R** ed and black
**S** ometimes, cars go fast.

**Scarlett Briston (5)**
Oakdale Primary School, Stanground

# Cars

**C** ars have wheels
**A** ll are round
**R** oll and move
**S** afe to drive on road.

## Dheeptha Manoj (5)
Oakdale Primary School, Stanground

# Boats

**B** oats can float
**O** n the water
**A** nd have sails
**T** o mermaid land.

## Mia Garwell (5)
Oakdale Primary School, Stanground

# Bus

**B** us is a vehicle
**U** se them to go to places
**S** ome are different colours.

## Amelie Monteforte (5)
Oakdale Primary School, Stanground

# Bus

**B** uses are like rainbows
**U** se them and get on
**S** ome are big.

## Erin Skipp (5)
Oakdale Primary School, Stanground

# Bus

**B** uses are big
**U** se them to travel
**S** ome are small.

## Molly Patten (5)
Oakdale Primary School, Stanground

# Autumn

I can hear the swaying trees, the noisy fireworks and the whistling wind,
I can smell the hot soup, the yummy marshmallows and the stinky leaves,
I can taste the hot soup, the dripping rain and the hot sausages,
I can see the yummy marshmallows, the speedy squirrels and the frightening fireworks,
I can feel the rough bark, the smooth leaves and the hard sweets.

## Jake Nicholson (7)
Penruddock Primary School, Penruddock

# Autumn

I can hear autumn leaves crunching under my feet as I walk along the wide path,
I can smell the sugary cake on the orange table,
I can smell pumpkin soup as well,
I can taste roast chicken with potatoes, yum, yum!
I can see trees gently swaying side to side as I walk along the path of leaves.
I can feel the bark on the trees and hot soup, ouch!

### Ella Platt (7)
Penruddock Primary School, Penruddock

# Autumn Feelings

**A** utumnal colours swirl in the wind
**U** nder the trees, the swift wind smells fresh
**T** he orange squirrels are camouflaged in the crunchy leaves
**U** tterly scrumptious hot cocoa is creamy in my mouth
**M** y jumper is as soft as a puppy's fur
**N** ice chicken soup sizzling in my mouth.

## Matilda (5)
Penruddock Primary School, Penruddock

# Autumn

I can see the swaying green trees,
I can see a brown, hard acorn,
I can see a colourful, pretty rainbow,
I can hear the leaves crunching under my feet,
I can hear the whistling wind next to my body,
I can hear hot, sizzling marshmallows,
I can taste some hot orange soup in my mouth.

## Eddie Seel (7)
Penruddock Primary School, Penruddock

# Autumn

I can hear the crunchy leaves,
I can see swaying trees,
I can taste yummy hot chocolate,
I can feel a sausage,
I can touch a cake at the food fair,
I can touch toffee apples at the food fair,
I can see a conker lying on the ground,
I can see a marshmallow on the campfire.

**Ted Ware (6)**
Penruddock Primary School, Penruddock

# Autumn

I can smell yummy soup, fresh pine cones, sausages, hedgehogs and water,
I can hear crunchy leaves, hard bark, rustling squirrels and swaying trees,
I can taste hot chocolate and soup,
I can see fireworks and popcorn,
I can feel the grass, sparklers and toffee.

## Dylan Offin (5)
Penruddock Primary School, Penruddock

# Autumn

In autumn, I can hear the crunchy leaves,
And the wind blowing wildly.
I can smell hot soup and the autumn barbecues,
I can taste roast dinners and autumn fruit,
I can see spiky conkers and red squirrels,
I can feel little acorns and tree bark.

**Lily-Ella Biggs (6)**
Penruddock Primary School, Penruddock

# Autumn

I can hear crunchy leaves and swaying trees,
I can smell hot cocoa, marshmallows, toffee and popcorn,
I can taste hot chocolate, apples and toffee apples,
I can feel the hard bark and hard conkers,
I can see fat squirrels bashing conkers.

## Ed O'Neil (7)
Penruddock Primary School, Penruddock

# Autumn

I can smell hot tomato soup, hot curry and hot vegetable soup,
I can hear the trees swaying and the leaves crunching under my feet,
I can taste my roast dinner and beans,
I can see all the different-coloured leaves,
I can feel wet leaves.

## Lewis Nicholson (5)
Penruddock Primary School, Penruddock

# Autumn

I can hear lovely swaying trees in the wind,
I can feel soft squirrels running across the woods,
I can smell burning hot soup in the bowl,
I can taste sausages on the barbecue,
I can see green and brown trees standing on the ground.

**Jordan Edmondson (6)**
Penruddock Primary School, Penruddock

# Autumn

I can hear crunchy leaves,
I can smell the fresh grass,
I can taste delicious sausages,
I can see green on the leaves,
I can feel rough sticks.

### Faith Fry (5)
Penruddock Primary School, Penruddock

# Autumn

I can smell yummy food,
I can hear rustling trees,
I can taste marshmallows,
I can see trees falling in the wind,
I can feel the rough bark.

## Jos Platt (6)
Penruddock Primary School, Penruddock

# Autumn

I can see acorns falling down,
I can hear squirrels in the trees,
I can smell hot chocolate,
I can feel soft leaves,
I can taste hot Vimto.

## Joseph Parker (6)
Penruddock Primary School, Penruddock

# Autumn

I can see glistening water,
I can hear the baby birds,
I can taste hot chocolate and soup,
I can smell apple pie,
I can see ladybugs.

## Isaac (6)
Penruddock Primary School, Penruddock

# London

- **L** ots of things to do
- **O** ut and about with friends
- **N** ever scam people (it's mean)
- **D** oing shopping with friends
- **O** yster cards to travel around
- **N** ight-time lights.

## Shiloh Marshall (8)
St Anthony's Catholic Primary School, Anerley

# Climate

In England, the temperature is sometimes cold,
And sometimes hot,
But in Nigeria, it is always hot.
Nigeria is always a hot country,
However, England, Nigeria and its people are awesome.

In England, the temperature is sometimes cold, and sometimes hot, Showcasing the four seasons not peculiar with tropical climates.
The seasons include spring, summer, autumn, and winter.
Because spring brings forth warmth, after the cold wet nights and between the sunshine heatwaves.
Because summer brings forth sunshine making flowers to blossom and be beautiful.
Because autumn makes people ready for the cold weather, early nights and slowly creeping to winter.
Because winter makes me happy as it approaches Christmas as well as the cold, wet and snowy days.
But in Nigeria, it is mostly hot with tropical air.
Nigeria is seen as a tropical country and the climate as well, which is common with many other tropical climates in Africa, the Caribbean, Asia, the Middle East, and some parts of the far east.

There are 3 major kinds of weather in Nigeria,
Rainy seasons, summer and Harmattan seasons.
Because rain brings forth cool and wet soils,
making plants grow much quicker.
Because the summer season brings forth sunshine
and a time to be merry on the beaches in Nigeria.
Because Harmattan makes the weather dry and
cold, like the winter season in other parts of the
world.
Our climates bring out the very best of each
country, regardless of the seasons.
From food to drinks, to dressing, housing and more
so our way of life.
So together let's join hands to protect our lovely
climate and planet; including both awesome
countries!

**Irentoluwa Murphy (7)**
St Anthony's Catholic Primary School, Anerley

# Autumn

The sounds of autumn:
The sound of rain on the window,
The fresh wind in the air,
And the booming noise of fireworks,
Driving my cat crazy.

The smells of autumn:
Bonfires on the 5th of November,
The smell of ash,
From burning leaves in your back garden,
It's a smell to remember.

The tastes of autumn:
Hot chocolate on a chilly day,
Eating apple pie on Halloween night,
Eating candy after trick-or-treating.

The feel of autumn:
Autumn feels spooky and creepy,
Everyone dressed as witches and ghouls,
And more amazing frights.

But most of all,
I'm excited about my birthday celebrations!

## Lola Harding (7)
St Anthony's Catholic Primary School, Anerley

# Young Writers Information

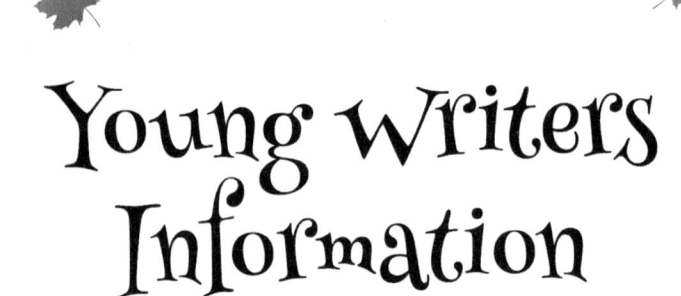

We hope you have enjoyed reading this book – and that you will continue to in the coming years.

If you're the parent or family member of an enthusiastic poet or story writer, do visit our website www.youngwriters.co.uk/subscribe and sign up to receive news, competitions, writing challenges and tips, activities and much, much more! There's lots to keep budding writers motivated!

If you would like to order further copies of this book, or any of our other titles, then please give us a call or order via your online account.

Young Writers
Remus House
Coltsfoot Drive
Peterborough
PE2 9BF
(01733) 890066
info@youngwriters.co.uk

Join in the conversation!
Tips, news, giveaways and much more!

YoungWritersUK    YoungWritersCW    youngwriterscw